LANCASHIRE TALES

Edited By Jenni Harrison

First published in Great Britain in 2017 by:

Young**Writers**
Est. 1991

Coltsfoot Drive
Peterborough
PE2 9BF
Telephone: 01733 890066
Website: www.youngwriters.co.uk

FOREWORD

Welcome Reader!

Are you ready to discover weird and wonderful creatures that you'd never even dreamed of?

For Young Writers' latest competition we asked primary school pupils nationwide to create a creature of their own invention, and then write a story about it using just 100 words – a hard task indeed! However, they rose to the challenge magnificently and the result is this fantastic collection full of battling aliens, lonely creatures and mischievous monsters causing havoc!

Here at Young Writers our aim is to encourage creativity in children and to inspire a love of the written word, so it's great to get such an amazing response, with some absolutely fantastic stories.

Not only have these young authors created imaginative and inventive creatures, they've also crafted wonderful tales to showcase their creations. These stories are brimming with inspiration and cover a wide range of themes and emotions - from fun to fear and back again!

I'd like to congratulate all the young authors in 'Crazy Creatures - Lancashire Tales' - I hope this inspires them to continue with their creative writing.

Jenni Harrison

CONTENTS

Rufus Knightley (7)	69
Isabelle Coulton (10)	70
Hannah Carter (8)	71
Evie Ormerod (8)	72
Calvin Watson (9)	73
Ellis Smith (9)	74
Mia Hackett (8)	75
Hannah Waite (7)	76
David Hall (8)	77
Libby Mari Anne Dunn (10)	78
Harry Dolan (7)	79
Poppy Di-Anne Mottershead (7)	80
Joseph Ward (9)	81
Chloe Lomax (7)	82
Aimee Haworth (8)	83
Jack Bobby Ashworth (7)	84
Lewis Walters (10)	85
Jake Hannay (9)	86
Meisha Gamble (10)	87
Daniel John Schofield (10)	88
Naomi Curness (8)	89
Samuel Zangoura (7)	90
Amy Jarvis (9)	91
Madelaine Beecham (10)	92
Grace Wilkinson (9)	93
Alannah Pollard (10)	94
Molly Kelly (8)	95
Harry Kendall (9)	96
Neve Grady (7)	97
Maddison Bleakley (7)	98
Alicia Holt (7)	99
Amelia Rose Watkins (9)	100
Phoebe Grace (8)	101
Evie Robinson (8)	102
Poppy Savage (9)	103
Harry Dean (9)	104
Lewis Alderson (8)	105
Ellie Jefferson (8)	106
Joshua Bailey (8)	107
Alexandros Berbatiotis (8)	108
Harry Clark (8)	109
Isabel Carter (9)	110
Natasha Greenwood (8)	111
Tom Turner (8)	112
Carter Michael Travers (10)	113
Henry Hughes (9)	114
Daniel Cowley (8)	115
Henry McRorie (8)	116
Evie Harrison (8)	117
Jasey Hartree (9)	118
Jake Bulpit (8)	119
Romilly Neve Doherty (7)	120
Isabella Dunn (8)	121
Archie Rowlands (7)	122
Mina Alice Boland (9)	123
Reuben Howe (7)	124
Evie Hargreaves (8)	125
Joseph Claxton (9)	126
Darcy Crook (7)	127
Alex Regan (8)	128
Isobel Ball (8)	129
Fred Hardwick (8)	130
Ocean Summer Flanagan (8)	131
Theo Francisco Madden (7)	132
Mason Hitchen (7)	133
Aaron Kershaw (8)	134
Heather Scott-Bates (8)	135
William John Nutter (7)	136
Isobel Lorna Bond (8)	137
Wil James Christian (9)	138
Jack Stubbs (9)	139
Owen Griffiths (7)	140
Lewis Robinson (7)	141
Joseph Simkin (8)	142
Daniel Clements (8)	143
Lydia Jane Lord (8)	144
Taylor Baker (8)	145

Rossall School, Fleetwood

Vismaya Pillai (10)	146

St Pius X Catholic Preparatory School, Preston

Shreya Tol (10)	147
Maryam Bapu (9)	148
Farwa Ali (10)	149
Edward Charles Greaves (9)	150
Amirah Master (9)	151
Rishan Ravishankar (9)	152
Aryan Patel (9)	153
Hadi Bawa (10)	154
Oliver Bamford (10)	155
Jonalisa Kubelabo (10)	156

St Stephen's CE Primary School, Blackburn

Aisha Patel (10)	157
Ahmad Phansa (10)	158
Alisha Surve (8)	159
Hafiza Bhamji (10)	160
Aliyah Bangi (10)	161
Aasiyah Patel (11)	162
Fatema Ibrahim Seedat (11)	163
Zain Ahmed (9)	164
Rozmina Patel (10)	165
Fatima Ravat (9)	166
Murtazah Shahzad (9)	167
Aisha Usman (9)	168
Zaid Kara (9)	169
Naailah Mubarakali (11)	170
Faiza Sheth (8)	171
Safwaan Ravat (9)	172
Zaynab Ravat (10)	173

THE STORIES

The Tale Of The Uncooked Dough

Slithering down the cobbled road came Pepperoni, his chilli pepper tail trailed behind him while the baron sun cooked his doughy skin. Burning... Sweating... Cooking. Cautiously fluttering his delicious chip wings at the smell of disgusting vegetables.

'This is nothing like my planet of Oosh-Kana-Bool-La-nu-to.' Instinctively, he launched his motion detectors onto the saturated floor. *Bang!* What was that? Creeping quietly was Christine, the carrot stick! But what she didn't know was that Pepperoni had inquisitive eyes on his swishing tail. Whipping its tail the beast launched his tail into Christine's head!

'That's how it's done! Which way is home?'

Sienna Curness (11)

Helmshore Primary School, Rossendale

Diamonds And Eagles

As skilled as champion warriors, Helios-Mutantos-Ouranos (Neptune) prowled stealthily over the grassy plains, his tail - as poisonous as a scorpion's - drooping. Alone... weary... nobody had his precious azure-blue diamond. Suddenly, he saw a darkish figure soaring above, the distinctive shape of an eagle. His fangs activated.

'Don't fear!' the eagle cawed, 'here's a jewel of lavish beauty!' A sapphire-like diamond glinted in the bird of prey's beak. Neptune leapt around screeching like he'd overdosed on coffee. His diamond had been found! Ox-like and as red as blood, his powerful wings beat viciously. Collecting it, he elegantly glided his way home.

Isabella Mary Owens (11)
Helmshore Primary School, Rossendale

Pillar-Strike's Mischief Magic

Scampering sneakily through weather control, mischievous Pillar-Strike invaded the planet Snowben. He zoomed to the control desk and rotated extreme heat (full)! Zipping to the nearest planet (where his magical mischief began). Scanning the area with his radar antennae he soon picked up an annoyance area. He quickly rocketed off with his falcon-like wings! He came across a strange looking building and snuck inside. What would he find now! Inside the building were different coloured lights dangling from the stairs! Suddenly he was surrounded! The king and his soldiers from Planet Snowben! 'Oh no!'
'You are under arrest mischievous Pillar-Strike!'

William Harding (10)
Helmshore Primary School, Rossendale

Mystery Monster

Giddy-Destroyer zoomed across the road in the boiling hot weather - short... strong... fast. Wiping sweat off his smooth forehead. Suddenly - *bang!* Realising he wasn't at home, as there was no cool summer breeze for starters. Looking around he tried to calculate his location using his super sonic eyes. He discovered he was two million miles away from home. Suddenly, he noticed a gigantic creature chasing him! Quickly, he activated his invisibility suit and sneaked around the enemy. Giddy-Destroyer pelted away from the beast. Luckily, he was tricking him now. Giddy-Destroyer had an advantage. Determinedly he defeated the gigantic creature. Yeah!

Charlie Waring (11)
Helmshore Primary School, Rossendale

Eyeball Adventure!

Eye-Destroyer slithered along on his four eyeballed feet - light orange, furry skin, emerald tentacles. Shivering violently, he glanced around him. This was nothing like home. No eyeballs available to eat. The crazy creature used his eyes on his wrinkly hands and legs to search around. Suddenly, he heard a whisper. A scary-looking creature surrounded him. Anxiously, he looked closer.

'Oh no, it's Devil Eyes!' As quick as a lightning bolt, Eye-Destroyer stomped away.

'Is this planet Eye Balls after all?' bellowed Eye Destroyer as he tried to get away from the mysterious monster. Will he escape the terrible creature?

Chloe Grace Stevenson (11)

Helmshore Primary School, Rossendale

Crontock's Crash To Chaos

Boom! Crontock's pod hurtled to the ground towards the derelict city. Crontock clambered out the pod, scanning the area for humans. Suddenly a figure appeared. It was Slipimenator! He was vacuuming the damaged remains of Crontock's pod.

'No!' he squealed. His energy had been drained, he couldn't get home. Slipimenator vanished, leaving Crontock with nothing. He ventured through the city to find life. Nothing! He used his thirteen eyes to help and soon came across a young toddler sucking all its energy but it wasn't enough. He soon collected damaged engines, but was it enough to get him back home?

Ava Baker (11)

Helmshore Primary School, Rossendale

Awakening From The Galaxy Above

'Get to work,' screamed the Monnottie as he shot his beaming lasers at the small aliens. Cackling, the Monnottie walked down to the dungeons, where Santa was locked up, as the monster had a cunning plan! Creeping silently, the curious monster strolled around unsuspecting houses on Christmas Eve, as he had teleported all the coal in the galaxy to Earth.

'Ahh, what a journey.' There she was, the Monnottie's mortal enemy, Talagifty.

'Argh!' shouted the monster as he woke the child up.

'Mum!' The child had startled the Monnottie so much that he ran away and was never seen again.

Lucia Kelly (11)

Helmshore Primary School, Rossendale

Pigy-Lick-A-Google's Adventures

Pigy-Lick-A-Google fluttered along her two gigantic purple, dragon-like wings. Feathery with smooth, yellow, slimy skin. She was shivering. She searched about. She realised this was nothing like home, no heat nor any sun. So Pigy-Lick-A-Google used her amazing two tongue skills to track where she was. Unexpectedly, she felt a tickle on her leg which went straight into a pinch. She looked on her leg. Nothing. 'Boo!' Right in front of her ruby eyes. Suddenly she found out it was Venomous Vampy Squirm smiling, showing his sharp teeth. 'Oh no!' shouted Pigy-Lick-A-Google, 'I have to get back home!'

Kaitlyn Watterson (10)
Helmshore Primary School, Rossendale

Jurassic World

There was a purple hybrid dinosaur. It could turn invisible. Once Megalosaurus got lost because he bumped his head. He went to the Antarctic from Washington DC but when he got back it was a park, by the name of Jurassic World. So the boss put Megalosaurus there. Another dinosaur called Indominus Rex followed. They battled. *Smash!* went a building. All the dinosaurs had a terrific battle. Megalosaurus turned invisible and rammed Indominus into the Megalodon enclosure. They heard nothing. Suddenly the horrifying Megalodon came up, scared them and ate Indominus. He was inside Megalodon, never seen on Earth again.

Austin Willis (7)
Helmshore Primary School, Rossendale

The Bad Dream

Quickly the Dream Demolisher clambered up the restless child's bed zealously rubbing his roaring, rumbling belly.

'This is going to be one of the biggest meals I've ever had,' screeched the Dream Demolisher, cautiously preparing to consume the dream and trade it for a nightmare until, *creak!* Uh oh, it was the Day Dream Doodler!

'Not you again.' The scrawny creature snatched his sticky pads, leaped to the floor where his enemy stood still as a pillar. In a single blink they were in a brutal fight, the mischievous Dream Snatcher shot out a fierce flaming fire laser beam! Dead!

Katie Jarvis (11)
Helmshore Primary School, Rossendale

Planet Sweet And Planet Chocolate

One dark and lonely night Chocolate Delight was awake. Chocolate Delight decided to break Lollipop Swirl's candy cane. Chocolate Delight stole the candy cane and decided to eat it all up. On the way back Chocolate Delight's spaceship broke down and he fell all the way to Earth. Lollipop Swirl found some red and white rock and made another candy cane. Suddenly Lollipop Swirl's body was complete changed: she had four lollipop eyes, two chocolate mouths, three carrot noses, two lollipop arms, two lollipop legs and one giant lollipop body coloured green, red, white and a beautiful light purple colour.

Yasmin Lodal (7)

Helmshore Primary School, Rossendale

The Water And Fire War

Uniblaze trotted swiftly beside the flame flowers. Huge wings flapped, whilst the fire burnt inside her horn. Flammable... furious... ferocious. Suddenly, she spotted a water corn, blue as the ocean. She came cantering by with a huge glistening wave behind her! Like a pool of blood, Uniblaze's eyes turned deep red. Furiously, she lit up like a wild fire and charged at the water corn, spreading fire as she went! The enemy carried on galloping. Flame turned to lava. After four tiring hours of fighting Uniblaze was the victor!
'Hip, hip hooray,' yelled Uniblaze, Planet Blaze was fiery once more!

Violet Addy (10)
Helmshore Primary School, Rossendale

The Creepily Crazy Adventures Of Bullbunny

Zooming like a rocket, Bullbunny shot out of the duke's house. His jewels had been tasty. As she bounded through the gutter, the rabbit ran into a sign. Bullbunny ignored the letters, but only saw the majestic pile of crown jewels. Suddenly a gust of wind caught her and flung Bullbunny onto the pavement.

'I need those jewels just as much as you, so let's go!' Bullbunny's arch-enemy, Foxature, cackled. As they climbed to the tower's window, they carefully squeezed in.

'Yoo hoo!' Foxature cried. As the weary guard turned his back, the rabbit smashed the glass and escaped...

Samantha Hampson (10)
Helmshore Primary School, Rossendale

Shape-Shifting Camouflager's Adventure

Slowly, the Shape-shifting Camouflager trudged along the rough road on his thin feet. He was as cold as ice! This was nothing like home, there was no soft sand for starters. Carefully the small creature quickly camouflaged into a large, broken oak tree. *Bang!* Suddenly, the Boggle Bum Catcher sprang out of a small bush nearby and threw a metal cage at the clearer creature. As fast as lightning the frightened monster unlocked an abandoned rose-red car with a sharp claw and scrambled in.

'Someone help,' shouted the monster. 'I definitely landed on the wrong planet again!'

Leah Darbyshire (11)
Helmshore Primary School, Rossendale

Fireball Mayhem

Do you know Screama-Fireball? He lives in Nashama (aka Lava Land).

One day he went for a fly; he thought all the other creatures were better than him, stronger, bigger and a lot braver. Something felt wrong, but what? The shadows closed around him, then he realised, he had flown far from Lava Land! Was he being followed?

'Arghh!' It was Singing-Waterfall. Screama hiccoughed and a fireball pouffed out of his mouth, singeing all Singing-Waterball's hair! He was totally bald and suddenly seemed very small. Screama-Fireball was now the greatest beast in all the land! 'Hooray!'

Heidi Caruana (11)
Helmshore Primary School, Rossendale

Ice Cream's Adventures On Planet Ping

Flying Ice Cream zipped along with her two wings flapping madly. Looking cute... colourful... curious, Ice Cream started to melt in the sizzling sun. Glancing around something caught her eye! *Bing!* An alarm sounded in her head - a mysterious creature like dazzling gold. She realised who it was! She stared at the awful and sly Sammy Spoonhead. The cheeky cone-like creature grabbed him angrily and zoomed upwards towards the stars. She wanted to drop him but she couldn't, he was stuck to her wing. Finally, he let go.
'No!' she announced. 'I'm not going back there again!'

Ellie-Grace Whittaker (11)
Helmshore Primary School, Rossendale

Hegechoc's Spaceship Adventure

Scampering through the dump, Hegechoc began to create his spaceship in hope to retreat back to Planet Chocolate. Hegechoc had failed his mission to find chocolate to keep his planet alive.

Assembling the parts to the spaceship, a gigantic spaceship landed.

'Oh no.' It was the planet's enemies, Planet Zog's Police Force. Using his powers Hegechoc turned invisible, he was nowhere to be seen. Suddenly Hegechoc transformed into his original form and scared off the enemies. He began his big quest to build a zooming spaceship. He would soon be zapping up back to Planet Chocolate.

George Claxton (10)

Helmshore Primary School, Rossendale

The Battle

Terribly Terrifying Timmy had travelled away from Terifactula just to battle it out with his enemy, the Magnificent Fluffy Dream Catcher. So they decided to go to a party to battle it out but little did he know the Magnificent Fluffy Dream Catcher had brought some friends along. What will go down... So the fight was on. Terribly Terrifying Timmy took down one of Magnificent Fluffy Dream Catcher's friends. He said to himself, 'One down, nineteen more to go.' And one by one he took all of Magnificent Fluffy Dream Catcher's friends down, including Magnificent Fluffy Dream Catcher as well.

Holly Eve Ashworth (10)
Helmshore Primary School, Rossendale

The Menacing Minotaur's Rescue Mission

The menacing Minotaur glitched in the room before shape-shifting into a book. She didn't know she wasn't on planet Duplon but didn't mind a bit. Soon, her worst enemies, Hairy Hairball and Ding Dong, entered whilst holding her best friend Gloopy Corn hostage. She waited for the best time then glitched closer and snatched Gloopy Corn with her marshmallow grabbing arms then zapped Hairy Hairball and Ding Dong. After that Gloopy Corn blew them off the face of the Earth! They both did their strange handshake then ate lots of popcorn and marshmallows filled with Gloopy Corn's rainbows!

Lizzy Barlow (9)
Helmshore Primary School, Rossendale

Bulzoar's Blast Of An Adventure

Bulzoar was a colour crazy creature with the ability to shoot gunk out of his tails and he could detach and re-attach his tails and shoot beams from his eyes.

Bulzoar climbed and jumped from a wild snake. Then he misjudged a jump and fell and both his tails came off and accidentally burnt Dom's snake.

'Argh, you killed my snake,' Dom the diddy man said.

'Run,' Bulzoar said. *Zap!* He zapped him with his heat beam eyes.

'Ow,' Dom said. 'This was not in the contract!'

Then Bulzoar used his tail gunk to pin him to a tree...

Alex Wilson (9)
Helmshore Primary School, Rossendale

Tranky Tree's Encounter

One day on an unknown planet, Tranky Tree was wandering through a forest when a human walked along. Hurriedly he jumped to the side and modified into an original Christmas tree, that was when the human walked off!

'Phew, that was close.' As he became himself again with his razor-sharp talons, up-lifting wings, and two terrifying horns. This wasn't Planet Forest, it was Earth! Suddenly one of the trees burst into flames! Out of a tree came the Inferno Devil. Instinctively, TT ran into a shuttle. It was just getting ready to set off. 'It's time!' he explained...

Mason Howarth (10)
Helmshore Primary School, Rossendale

The Terrifying Story Of Mr Clumsy Rocket Monster

Mr Clumsy Rocket Monster felt injured - he stumbled with his smooth, spongy, turquoise body. Feeling hot (so was the sand) he shot upwards with his jet boosted pack. But he crashed into a spindly tree, bounced off, then hit the ground. Accidentally he shut down his rockets. Mr Clumsy Rocket Monster scanned into the distance and noticed a grey cloud full of lightning bolts. Out of nowhere a metal, evil robot jumped towards him and started diving menacingly towards him. Mr Clumsy Rocket Monster thought to himself, *oh no! This is nothing like my home planet, Zarog, nothing at all!*

Alex Sagar (10)
Helmshore Primary School, Rossendale

Bunny Rainbow Teeth And His Lost Tooth

Bunny Rainbow Teeth hopped along the windy park path. He was looking for some carrots and his friends. Finally, he found some carrots and his friends. They all enjoyed their carrots, but *crunch!* 'Ow!' Bunny Rainbow Teeth yelped.
'You've lost your blue tooth,' his friends chorused. Suddenly, his gummy gap grew a new sparkly and shiny blue tooth. 'Wow!' they all said.
'That's amazing!' said Long Tongue Toe. *What a cool trick*, he thought. So from now on if he loses a tooth, it's not a problem for Bunny Rainbow Teeth.

Melissa Noblett (8)
Helmshore Primary School, Rossendale

The Adventurous Journey

Cotton Candy set off to her planet. After her journey Cotton Candy decided she had reached her planet and so she landed the ship. But something wasn't right, something seemed weird! Cotton Candy felt herself melting and frying in the heat.

'This definitely isn't home,' she said. Lots of things were brown and runny. Suddenly she felt a shadow fall over her... It was Dark Chocolate! But, don't worry, soft, cuddly Cotton Candy knew karate.

'I don't like you,' and she beat him up. Cotton Candy flew back to her planet. Pink Cotton Candy was back!

Katie Knowles (8)
Helmshore Primary School, Rossendale

Zorborg And The Mystery Planet

Bang, there were explosions everywhere on Planet Flap as the Sprachers invaded, and everyone was shrinking from the bug spray. Eventually, Planet Flap inflated, then poor Zorborg was shot like a bullet through space, unconscious. He saw himself flying to a mystery planet, covered with blue and it had green bits. Zorborg landed softly on the goop, we started to use his abilities to walk on liquids but a grey arrow with a mouth swam towards him and he began to run. Zorborg collapsed painfully to the ground and wondered what was next. What was he going to do?

Owen Rhodes (11)
Helmshore Primary School, Rossendale

Eyeless Jerry Breaks Free

Eyeless Jerry stomped through the muddy green park with his giant feet, because he wanted to scare people and go, 'Boo, boo, boo!' Suddenly he tripped over a large pebble and his eye fell off his head.

'Ahhh,' and it hurt, but then a police van appeared. They threw Eyeless Jerry and his eyeball into the van. Eyeless Jerry got put in handcuffs.

'No!' he shouted but he figured out it was his arch enemy Bog Tog Turtle. The Bog Tog Turtle put Eyeless Jerry's handcuffs into a machine. There was an awful racket. Eyeless Jerry broke his hands free.

Ethan Edwards (8)
Helmshore Primary School, Rossendale

The Colourful Crazy Creature's Adventure

The colourful, crazy creature crawled along with his three tails and a body as hairy as a orangutan. Sweating madly in the scorching weather, tiring with his razor-sharp claws. This beast looked around, checking where he was with his large twelve eyes. There were no castles or creatures like his home in a place called Dangerous. Not even any caves to sleep in like he would. Surprisingly, he identified the Deadly Destroyer circling him, causing mayhem, trying to hurt him with his sharp claws. Then the crazy creature whacked his terrifying tail at him then flew away to find home.

Jay MacGeachie (10)
Helmshore Primary School, Rossendale

Amazing World Of Alien Santa

Jiggley Alien Santa tiptoed through the cold, scary factory. It was quiet because everyone was protecting the factory. Jiggley Alien Santa was looking for a gem that can explode. An evil policeman handcuffed Alien Santa to a monster machine. Suddenly the handcuff got stuck to an lever. Rip went Alien Santa's hand. Alien Santa escaped. Jiggley Santa ran and banged his face on the sharp edge of the glass case. Just then he saw his enemy with a sharp sword. Alien Santa broke the glass case and snatched the gem. Scared, he ran out of the factory saying, 'Phew, hooray!'

William Aderemi Yinusa (8)

Helmshore Primary School, Rossendale

Flat Snogo

Snogo stomped through the green, grassy park on his big and small feet. It was a gorgeous day when Snogo was on the hunt for bogies. Suddenly, Snogo tripped up and got stuck to the ground. Then Tissue Man picked him up and stuck him to the tree. When Snogo woke up he heard Tissue Man saying, 'Why are you flat?'

'I'm not flat!'

'Yes you are flat.'

'Are you kidding?'

'No, I'm not, Snogo!' said Tissue Man.

What am I going to do to get rid of it.

The next day Snogo awoke and he wasn't flat.

Brandon Cockerill (8)
Helmshore Primary School, Rossendale

Freezeboy's Adventure

Freezeboy hadn't a clue where he was because he had been lost for the third day alone. This strange creature looked extremely crazy. Altogether he has seventeen eyes, six are big and eleven are small. Goggl Bobbl has the most strange mouth you'll ever see. For one split second Goggl Bobbl decided to look up. Suddenly, a fiery, red creature turned up and spoke out, 'Do you wanna know each other?' Freezeboy didn't answer and hovered off. Goggl Bobbl wondered about him and wanted to find out more about him. He discovered he could help him get to his home.

Robert Barton (10)
Helmshore Primary School, Rossendale

Big Mac's Enormous Adventure

Slowly Big Mac halted, he was scorching, the cheese sweat drooling down his 39 eyes. Then Big Mac stopped and looked around, this was nothing like home! There was no food for starters, eyeing around Big Mac realised he was at Meatball Mountain, which is a precise heat level to cook the scrumptious sausages and mesmerising meatballs. Then a loud noise cluttered by.

'Who goes there?'

'Ha, ha.' His arch-enemy Hot Dog Steve shot out of nowhere then the two meaty foods had an all-out battle, hit after hit, until finally Big Mac finished Steve off!

Dylan Jones (11)

Helmshore Primary School, Rossendale

Super Star Stamper's Great Adventure

As big as a tower, Super Star Stamper stamped along in the icy terrain. Shivering... tired... scared. The ugly beast walked slowly with his arms clinging on behind him. Super Star Stamper scanned the whole inter space for food and enemies, but all he could see was ice and water. Where were all of the mountains, rivers and waterfalls? This was nothing like home. *Voom! Crash! Bang! Wallop!* The army with security pigs were running for Super Star Stamper. Quickly, he hid. Will he ever get out of this alive? This is a dangerous situation to be in. 'Oh no!'

Dominic Morton (10)
Helmshore Primary School, Rossendale

Flames' Adventures With King Kong

Flames strutted into his party. He was eleven years old today and was feeling like the happiest alien living on Jupiter. The only person who could spoil his fantastic day was King Kong. He was Flames' enemy and lived on the planet Venus. Everybody on Jupiter was having a great time dancing, singing and eating Burger King. Then, without warning, King Kong crashed through the wall, destroying everything in his path. Flames was furious! He jumped into action as quick as lightning. Using his magic powers he made King Kong disappear in a flash, never to be seen again.

Rory Finn Ainscough (11)

Helmshore Primary School, Rossendale

The Tales Of The Trolls

Calmly the fluffy muffy troll was skipping happily along when, strangely, a sudden shiver ran up his veins. He had brown, silky skin... rainbow teeth and butterfly wings. He looked around, it looked nothing like home, where was the dismal, dark tree? Suddenly a very funny shadow emerged. It looked like a vegetable. Was it his arch-enemy, Bob the broccoli. He was back! The crazy creature was as small as an ant and Bob the broccoli was as big as an elephant! He decided to fight, *whizz! Bam!* Bob the broccoli used his special move. 'Oh no!' he screamed.

Stephen Lees (10)
Helmshore Primary School, Rossendale

The Lemonade Lover!

Plodding steadily, Fantastic Fizz Pop Wallop Bang was strolling down Lemonade Land when he spotted a colossal park, which was as big as the Titanic ship! He played on the super swings, slippery slides, the wobbly roundabout and the zig zaggy zipwire. Until he spotted his fizzy lemonade was being drunk by Fiery Fireblob, his worst enemy. He zoomed over as Fiery Fireblob charged straight away to the lemonade river with seven bottles of lemonade in his hands and poured them straight into the river. Everyone was sad but they all had a swim and lived happily ever after!

Ruby Nuttall (9)
Helmshore Primary School, Rossendale

The Mission To Save Home

Slitherborg zoomed through the air scanning for bits of metal to build his new spaceship. He needed the formula to save his planet from destruction. Assembling parts with his super-sticky web, it was soon finished. His detector told him the formula was underground. He dug relentlessly for ages until finally he hit a huge golden box, he pulled it out and cracked it open. There it was, the formula to save his planet. But before he could take off, his arch enemy Dinoshark shot out steaming acid, Slitherborg tangled him in unbreakable web. He then shot up into the sky.

Harry Sneddon (11)
Helmshore Primary School, Rossendale

My World Of Nyan Cat

Nyan Cat happily skipped gracefully across the beautiful moonshine moor with lots of spots and planets, Mars, Milky Way and so on. Suddenly Nyan Cat tripped and she came back up and she was going faster and faster.

'I'm flying, I'm flying so high like a diamond in the sky.' Then she swooped down and scratched and scratched the pixel dogs in the rocket ships. Nyan Cat defeated them.

'Something's creeping up on me,' whispered Nyan Cat. 'Ahhh,' shouted Nyan Cat, 'it is the ruler of the pixel dogs.'

Molly Flair Flanagan (8)

Helmshore Primary School, Rossendale

The Story Of Pingpongpiddlypong

Once upon a time, many moons ago, there was a small, green, furry creature with rabbit ears, he could breathe purple fire, and shoot fire bombs out of his finger tips. His name was Pingpongpiddlypong. He grew bee wings when he needed to fly.

One day he came across Dipaldocusbob, his enemy, they hated each other so much they went into war. Dipaldocusbob shot ice at him, and Pingpongpiddlypong shot fire bombs at him. They both got wounded badly. Dipaldocusbob was sitting by a lava pit to warm his feet, Pingpongpiddlypong crept up behind him. *Splash!*

Ellysia Shannon-Wallace (9)
Helmshore Primary School, Rossendale

The Fluffy Dreamcatcher

Allow me to introduce you to the Fluffy Dreamcatcher... Far away in Cloud Cuckoo Land. Tired, it slowly opened its two green and purple eyes. Suddenly she climbed out of her puffy cloud to brush her pink, candyfloss-like fur, when she smelt her prey. She crept up to the end of the gigantic, white, fluffy cloud and swept through the big, fluffy clouds, then jumped... Flying, she steadied herself. Eventually she reached the brown, crooked, mouldy door and peered through it. 'Mmmm, nice, tasty dreams.' And with that she swept and caught them! So watch out!

Alicia Joy Quinn Jones (9)
Helmshore Primary School, Rossendale

Spike's Super Journey

Spike soared across the azure sky with his wings as red as a rose drifting in the wind. Spiky... chubby... colourful skin. Sweltering badly, he heard a strange noise; saw an illuminated, giant shadow with his invisibility, he made himself disappear so no one could identify him. Suddenly, the figure leaped out a bristly brush and it was... the dark, deadly dog with his assistant Cowardly Cat! They had found him after 30 years.

After a while they left, but to be on the safe side he stayed invisible so he carried on with his fabulous and adventurous journey!

Kali Boddy (10)
Helmshore Primary School, Rossendale

Mr Stink Bomb's Life

Mr Stink Bomb stomped through the forest whilst trumping, 'Oops!' Mr Stink Bomb stomped out of the forest before some trees fell down on him. 'Oh, I'm sorry, I forgot to tell you my name, my name is Mr Stink Bomb!' He smelt like a skunk and Mr Stink Bomb was like a bowl full of jelly. He could walk into trees and he didn't hurt himself. Anyway, that doesn't matter. He just came out of the forest but he didn't know where he was. He could see a crazy creature in the green grass, it was Mr Bowling Ball...

Ryan James Hanson (8)
Helmshore Primary School, Rossendale

Jeff The Wrecker

Jeff woke up because he'd had nightmares. He walked around eating anything. He had fluffy ears, a unicorn horn and sometimes grew three tongues. He ate everything in sight and even bit into building, although they were mud! They tasted horrible so he swapped onto cars.

Suddenly, Bob the beetle came out and tried to stop him. He tried to block off everything Jeff tried to eat, so Jeff used his three tongues to eat Bob. With a crunch, Bob cracked into pieces. After that, Jeff had to get new teeth because his old ones rotted away into tiny pieces.

William Holroyd (9)

Helmshore Primary School, Rossendale

World Of Monsters

Once upon a time, there lived a monster named Skittles. Every night she went to scare people. She was hungry most of the time. She really loved sweets and sugary food especially marshmallows. Skittles loved to fly very high in the sky wearing pink and purple clothes and had bright green skin. One day Skittles was flying to a castle in the clouds when a hungry monster with black fur appeared. The monster wanted to eat Skittles because she was sweet and sugary. Skittles used her super sugar powers to magic a sugar sword and she killed the black monster!

Alexia Holmes (7)
Helmshore Primary School, Rossendale

Dragonoid's Return...

Blazeristous is a three-headed blue monstrous dragon-like creature with a scorpion tail that shoots lava beams, he also has feet that do this too. Blazeristous soared over the dark, haunting forest using his large, spiked wings.

It was a dark, gloomy day when Blazeristous was searching for magical items and then he saw his enemy. He went flying forwards but crashed into a giant, hard oak tree and was knocked out. When he awoke he found six magical items. Unfortunately, his enemy wasn't far behind so he attacked Blazeristous and stole his items...

Monty Howarth (8)
Helmshore Primary School, Rossendale

The Adventures Of Crazy Cake Katie

Crazy Cake Katie was an unusual cake. Pluto's home to over a thousand cakes, but Katie was different to everyone else. She used to live on Earth with her beautiful best friend, Toffee Ice Cream. Now Katie and her long-lost best friend were worst enemies, they'd hated each other since Katie moved to Pluto. Katie turned around and saw dreadful news standing right in front of her... Toffee Ice Cream. Oh no. What was she doing here? She was angry. Very angry. Katie charged towards her enemy, pushed her the edge of the planet, never to be seen again.

Zahra Lodal (10)
Helmshore Primary School, Rossendale

The Battle Of Zen And Banker

One lovely day on Carzea, (a very weird planet compared to Earth), Banker, the blue mechanical Minotaur, was stamping along the crimson road rolling his eye, he was extremely bored. Suddenly, Zen, the master shape-shifter, flew down from the sky.

'Argh!' screamed Banker as he fell to the ground. It was Zen's troops that shot a net at him and pinned him to the ground. But then Banker used his super strength to break out but Zen was already on the run. Banker flew to save the citizens from the fire that Zen started. Then he stopped Zen!

Lewis Griffiths (10)

Helmshore Primary School, Rossendale

Spiky-Star's Adventure

Spiky-Star stomped through Fangy Town on his two big feet. It was a miserable, rainy day and Spiky-Star was trying to steal money, gold, diamonds and food. Because Spiky-Star is stealing a lot of jewels the Boretto dragons are after him. Two years on he was just about to buy a house when the Boretto dragons arrived called Bernard and Edward. Suddenly, he shape shifted into a piece of grass. Edward and Bernard looked around to see if Spiky-Star was around anywhere. Will the Boretto dragons get him or will Spiky-Star get in jail forever?

Benjamin Watterson (9)
Helmshore Primary School, Rossendale

Lightning Saves The Day

Lightning swung along with his three blue tentacles, he was like a block of ice. 'There's no way this is Griffany!' There were no earthworms for starters. His mane was blowing in the cold, icy wind. Then suddenly there was a rumble and a grumble and the ice cracked! Lightning had an idea but he needed help, so he summoned his friend Sally. Together they shot the ice with their magnet lightning and used it to close the crack. Then he swung home to Griffany to play with Sally and all of his friends, they were best friends.

Olive Barnard (7)
Helmshore Primary School, Rossendale

Cyborg-Falcon, The Dream Stealer

Rocketing down to Earth, the Cyborg-Falcon was scorching as he fell through the Earth's atmosphere. Once landed, softly he crept silently into a girl's bedroom. Using his dream changer skills, he tried to change dreams to nightmares. Suddenly from out of the shadows came his enemy, Nutrilizer, trying to stop him. Using his laser beam eyes he escaped quietly. Will he be back again? Will he be able to tell his strict commander that he had failed his mission to make a little girl's dream become a nightmare of hell? And can he own up to it?

Ethan Willis (10)

Helmshore Primary School, Rossendale

Fire Feet's Lucky Find!

Rumble, rumble, Fire Feet bounced along searching for some breath. Suddenly he spotted a family of six devouring their dinner. Dropping onto the roof of the semi-detached house, he clambered through the striped window to find the Ice King (his enemy), freezing the youngster's bed. The Ice King noticed him, but he had already melted the bunk. Fire Feet jumped down and used his laser eyes to zap the Ice King. As quick as a flash he cried, 'Stop, don't hurt me. I will return to my home planet - Pluto.'

Jack Hanson (10)
Helmshore Primary School, Rossendale

Fobble-Ogg The Monster

One bright, sunny day, Fobble-Ogg happily skipped down the path on Planet Bing-Bong. His orange, spongy skin boiling in the sun (it was a lot hotter on his planet today than usual). Suddenly, he spotted something crusty with blueberries on top. It was his mortal enemy, Google-Eye Blueberry Pie Face! Pie Face grabs pies out of his pockets and chucks them at his victims. Fobble-Ogg thought with the brain for a belly button. He threw his spiky fur balls at his opponent. They started to fight, then laugh. They decided to be friends! Until next time...

Orla Douglas (10)
Helmshore Primary School, Rossendale

The Transformation

Pikachu was walking to meet his friends at the park one day when he slipped and fell into some slime and banged his head.

'Ouch!' he said, then suddenly he transformed into a slimy version of himself. Then a very sly grin crept up on Slimy Pikachu's face. Slimy Pikachu ran to the park and scared his friend, Slimy Pikachu smiled as he thought about him scaring the whole world and becoming famous! When it was time to go home Slimy Pikachu walked home, smiling all the way and scaring people, Slimy Pikachu was very, very happy.

Carmen Carter (10)

Helmshore Primary School, Rossendale

The Evil Siblings

Bigglebomb flew down to Earth to a hot and sandy desert. Bigglebomb was walking. He turned a corner and he saw his evil brother, Bombbiggle and his evil sister Miggleboom. His brother and sister were surprisingly working as a team, they were on a mission to kill Bigglebomb. He knew he had to get away but he couldn't because those two were there, he only has one way to get away. Bombbiggle and Miggleboom were getting out their space busters so he had to think fast, he used his stink bomb fart then lasered them and thankfully he got away.

Noah Yates (10)
Helmshore Primary School, Rossendale

Pretty Fangs' Fluffy, Puffy, Pink Palace

Pretty Fangs lived in the fluffy, puffy, pink palace. She was half blue and half purple with a zig zag tail and big, bright green eyes. The palace was next to a pink, colossal volcano.

One day it erupted and hot lava pushed down the volcano pouring on the palace. Pretty Fangs sprinted outside.

'Oh no,' shouted Pretty Fangs. She decided to use her power of freezing to stop the lava. It took half an hour to stop the lava. Pretty Fangs saved the fluffy, puffy, pink palace. Everyone was cheerful so they had a massive disco party.

Millie Waring (9)
Helmshore Primary School, Rossendale

The Enemies' Meeting

The silly, kooky monster arrived back from his home planet, Kooker. When he arrived he trudged through his cave with his small, bare feet. Then he suddenly heard a noise, he turned around. It was his worst enemy. The funny, fiery monster, he wanted to fight the fiery monster so he jumped at him. Apparently, he just wanted to play so they went into the forest next to the cave and started to play with each other's powers. Surprisingly, they had a lot of fun and were very merry together and they were best friends and were always best friends!

Maia Dirjan (9)
Helmshore Primary School, Rossendale

The Battle

Hideous Hairy Huble Google-Eye, zoomed down from Planet Star Space in his spaceship full of gadgets, full of things he needs to defeat his worst enemy, Hairy Fireball Splat. That day he came down to planet Earth to try and defeat Hairy Fireball Splat, who made trouble wherever he goes and invaded Star Space. When he got down to Planet Earth he found Fireball Splat. He spat out fireballs and Goggle-Eye shape-shifted into a fireball, flew towards Fireball Splat killing him instantly! Then Google-Eye went back to his home planet and had a party!

Imogen Grundy (9)
Helmshore Primary School, Rossendale

Moustache Maniac's Adventures

Moustache Maniac trudged along on two twig-like feet. His rough blue skin was melting in the heat of the land. Exploring for hours, he teleported all around the place until he came to a Monster High School. Marching, he went into a class and found the Devilish Cyclone who looked ferocious. He ran from his desk and started chasing Moustache Maniac. Soon he caught up with him and threw him into the sea. But he grabbed onto the Cyclone with his super long moustache, grabbed himself back to the Cyclone, who chased him back to the sea in his palm.

Joshua Lowthion (10)
Helmshore Primary School, Rossendale

Scareshanks And The Robbery Rumble

Sneaking silently, Scareshanks slipped his soft, squishy body through the door of house thirteen. Silence. All of a sudden he started to wonder if anybody was in. *Creak!*
'What was that?' The unidentified object started to slide suspiciously. He knew something was wrong. Robbers! Dashing heroically, he charged to take down the vicious victim, only to find his evil enemy Flyclops devouring and raiding all the cupboards in search of food. In an instant, his red-hot laser eye shot Flyclops out of existence. Would he return?

Matthew Bolton (10)
Helmshore Primary School, Rossendale

Oh No

Fubber Dubber soared through the skies of Paris using his four wings, trying to find a portal to the candy castle. It was a beautiful day. Fubber Dubber crashed into the Eiffel Tower and his leg fell off, so he went to surgery for seven weeks and had a new technical, shiny, robotic leg but it didn't work!

Fubber Dubber got a hair do, a low aircap and some braces. I wonder why? Oh I know why, it's to impress his king... he eventually found the portal, he went through and found himself in a spooky, dark, horrible candy forest.

Harry John Lord (9)

Helmshore Primary School, Rossendale

Weird Adventure

Rainbow Day was a colourful and bright pony. She poops ice cream and rainbows when she's happy. Rainbow Day had been driving along then she crashed! She landed on an island in the middle of nowhere. Rainbow Day wanted to go but she couldn't. So she got out her things and made an enormous bouncy castle! It was so big that five elephants could jump on it! Then it burst, it was so floppy that she lassoed her planet and brought it down. She was so happy to meet her friends that she pooped rainbows and yummy chocolate ice cream!

Freya Lax (8)
Helmshore Primary School, Rossendale

Tentington

Tentington was like jelly. He was as blue as bubblegum and loved slithering around. Tentington slithered around the ice rink, he was trying to find a way to get onto the ice, without slipping. Suddenly, Parrot Plongano flew straight towards him. Parrot Plongano was Tentington's worst enemy! Tentington ran as fast as his tentacles could carry him but unfortunately he fell! He turned round and Parrot Plongano came to the ground. Tentington quickly made a gun shape with his tentacles. He shot Parrot Plongano and Parrot Plongano died...

Emma Stubbs (9)
Helmshore Primary School, Rossendale

Discovering Two Legs

Fluffy Wuffy Ding Dong was in Planet Fluffy Land and she was going to the fluff museum and she accidentally teleported to Fluff Boggler's Boggle Land and she couldn't teleport back because she was out of energy and Fluff Bogglers ran at her and she couldn't run fast because she had four legs. One runs left, one runs right and one runs back and one goes forward. So then she jumped up and when she landed she had two legs. She ran away and got her energy back and teleported back to Fluffy Land and never, ever teleported again.

Bella Nuttall (9)
Helmshore Primary School, Rossendale

The Mosquito Frog

There once was a mosquito frog. He (who could be a she) had no name. He is quite cheeky because he jumps on people's backs which make them itchy for the rest of the year. The mosquito frog was going to do it to the president today but he got noticed and the president had mosquito spray! The mosquito frog hopped away then went straight back into the room and hopped onto the president's hand, that got itchy and he dropped the spray. Then the mosquito frog jumped on the president's back, that also got itchy. It was successful.

Harrison Smith (9)
Helmshore Primary School, Rossendale

Eagle Over The Woods

Sticky Stick was stomping through the brown forest with light green leaves on is stick-like feet. It was a sunny day when Sticky Stick was trying to find a luxury home. Sticky Stick was being followed by a giant brown eagle, he hid behind a tree and camouflaged himself. Then the bird didn't know where Sticky Stick was so the bird flew away. Then he ran home as fast as his legs would take him. Finally, he watched the brown giant eagle fly away so after that he went straight to sleep when he walked into his nice, comfy bedroom.

Harry Darbyshire (8)
Helmshore Primary School, Rossendale

Rekunic's Casa Catastrophe

Once on Jupiter Rekunic's poisonous talons gripped the ground. It had been a long 20 years on Jupiter and it was time to give birth. He had to make sure that his egg had a Casa baby inside and not an organism called Ramsteriam. He squeezed. Finally an egg came out. Purple spots, check. Green spots, check. Time for X-ray; Ramsteriam-free! Rekunic went for a stroll but when he returned he realised the egg had changed colour to yellow - that was a sign of Ramsteriam! He found his dagger and plunged it into the egg. Then he was safe.

Benedict Milnes (7)
Helmshore Primary School, Rossendale

Mr Weird's Wacky World

Mr Weird woke up and toppled out of bed. He was a rainbow monster who had small, beady eyes, but he realised he couldn't fly. *Uh oh*, he thought. Luckily, he knew a place to go, but before anything happened he was taken away. When he woke up he was in Dreamland. Then he stumbled over to a pink unicorn with a white mane. His legs started to tremble and all of a sudden, *poof!* The pink unicorn turned into a green alien. But Mr Weird's horn was tingling with fright. Out of nowhere Mr Weird vanished into thin air!

Ella Rose Duckworth (8)
Helmshore Primary School, Rossendale

Not Big Enough

Suddenly, Bing Bing saw his worst enemy, Trick Trample. For some peculiar reason he was so much bigger than him and he was not pleased! As quick as a flash he remembered that every eight years one growth potion appears somewhere in the mighty river, in the spectacular jungle. So he set off on his magical journey to find the potion of growth. He shifted into a fish with arms and poured into the river. Suddenly a bright light appeared. So that's where he headed. He drank the potion, shot back up and saw Trick Trample running away!

Dale Ryan Lomax (9)
Helmshore Primary School, Rossendale

Revenge From Alfie

Perat Person was a rat with wings and a long tongue. He flew to his island, Ratops.
One day he was about to go outside when a rock hit his head, it was a rock from an alien called Alfie. Aflie is Perat Person's enemy and this time he wants to kill Perat Person. So he decided to go to Africa but then, *smack!* Alfie hit Perat Person with a rock. Then Alfie's friend comes but he's tougher than Alfie so Perat Person turns into Alfie's friend, defeats Alfie and returns to Ratops with a cheer from his family.

Luke Gregory Brierley (8)
Helmshore Primary School, Rossendale

Fluff Versus Flack

In Winky Dinky Town, the best town ever, Fluffy the cloud man had powers like laser beam hands, invisibility and vampire teeth. He wore a top hat, had a walking stick and huge eyes.
One day in Winky Dinky, Fluff's worst enemy Flack wanted a battle. So they did, it lasted for five days. On the last day they were so weak, but oh no, Flack was winning. He tried to punch Fluff, but he stuck in his teeth and Flack disappeared. The town loved Fluff so much they had the biggest party ever. Fluff became famous, hooray for Fluff.

Rufus Knightley (7)
Helmshore Primary School, Rossendale

The Flame Monster Vs Dr Water Ball

The flame monster was running as fast as lightning through the wet jungle. He'd crashed his space car in this place. The ground wasn't burning like at home. Just then the flame monster's enemy was standing in front of him. Dr Water Ball! The war was on! Dr Water Ball threw a water ball at the flame monster, he threw one back. The flame monster shot poison from his eyes. He fired back. In a flash the water ball had disappeared. He was gone! He wandered around. His space car! He fixed it and flew back home to the sun!

Isabelle Coulton (10)

Helmshore Primary School, Rossendale

Black Beast And The Broken Ship

One day there was a smash and a black beast came out of the smoke with razor teeth and manta ray stinging tentacles. The funniest thing is the black beast's name was Black Beast. Funny right? But he was lost in London, one of the biggest cities ever. How was he going to get home? He looked round, couldn't see any of his favourite restaurants. He looked round again, he said to himself, 'I can fix the ship.' He went to the shops and bought the stuff he needed and the ship was fixed and he soon zoomed off happily.

Hannah Carter (8)

Helmshore Primary School, Rossendale

Gog And Earth

A long time ago there lived a planet called Pop. On the planet lived a monster called Gog. One day Gog was floating in space and crashed into Earth. 'Wow, I've never visited Earth,' he said, 'but I do miss space.'
A while later his friends were wondering where Gog was. One saw a hole in Earth. 'Oh no, he crashed into Earth, let's save him.'
'Good idea,' Hog said. Soon Gog go hungry but something darkened the sky, he looked to the right and saw his friends and went back home!

Evie Ormerod (8)
Helmshore Primary School, Rossendale

Trickster Trample

Trickster Trample was running across an alleyway out-running a train and then into a jungle filled with sand. Trickster Trample laid down with his tail pointing upwards, at that moment he saw Bing Bong, his enemy. He pulled him over and teleported into a tree. Trickster Trample had had enough of his enemies so he teleported to him and pushed him off into a bush and super sped away, but couldn't stop so ended up in the busiest building on Planet Pempel and he didn't stop running into the wall, for two weeks non-stop!

Calvin Watson (9)
Helmshore Primary School, Rossendale

The Story Of Big Mouth Hoopa

Big Mouth Hoopa came from a planet called Crazy Planet Zooloob.

One day Big Mouth Hoopa wanted to know what space looked like so he built a massive rocket to go to space; he thought it was awesome. Until he fell into Mars. When he hit the ground his enemy was surrounding him. Big Mouth Rainer made Hoopa's mouth big by freezing him. That's why he is called Big Mouth Hoopa. Hoopa fixed his robot and went back to his planet, Crazy Planet Zooloob. The Zooloobs were all crying until the Big Mouth Hoopa came back.

Ellis Smith (9)
Helmshore Primary School, Rossendale

Doubble Colour Monster

Doubble Colour Monster has four arms and six legs and is purple, orange, chubby and colourful. Suddenly he tripped over a huge rock and all of his seven eyes fell out. In just a second, a huge lump appeared and Doubble Colour Monster rubbed and rubbed but it didn't go away.

After a couple of days, it grew bigger and he tried putting cream on but it didn't work and after going to the doctor it still didn't work. In a puff it grew back. That's how he discovered that he could grow eyes again.

Mia Hackett (8)

Helmshore Primary School, Rossendale

Abbingong's Mistake

Abbingong was in his spaceship driving back home to his planet, Bingonpo, a sweet planet with a chocolate sea and candy cane trees. Abbingong was the friendliest creature in the world! He was nice and kind and he had orange skin and wings. Then he landed on the planet. 'Uh oh!' He had landed on his enemy's planet! Now what to do? Then he was dead. His friends came and zapped him alive again. Then his friends said, 'We've got tickets for the unbelievable magic show!' 'Yippee, yippee!'

Hannah Waite (7)
Helmshore Primary School, Rossendale

The Big Fight!

Once upon a time, there was a monster called Red Fiery Shadow. He lived underground and he was very scary and Red Fiery Shadow went to an underground lake in a cave. He found a big dead sea monster and skinned it to eat it! He also found an octopus which was alive. The octopus swam up to Red Fiery Shadow and tried to strangle him but Red Fiery Shadow used his magic powers and killed the evil octopus with fire! Red Fiery Shadow carried the dead octopus home and ate it up for tea! He had sweets for pudding!

David Hall (8)

Helmshore Primary School, Rossendale

Pika's Stinger

One day, Pika's enemy took his sting away from his tail! Pika did know someone who could fix it for him, and that person was Bigglebob. He was like a wizard who saved everyone! So Pika slid his way there. He got there and Bigglebob said to dip the tail in lava. And so he did. Pika's tail had sparks coming out of it. He touched Bigglebob and it stung him hard! Pika and Bigglebob were so happy! Off Pika and Bigglebob went for revenge on the evil creature. Bigglebob with Pika's cute ears waving in the wind...

Libby Mari Anne Dunn (10)
Helmshore Primary School, Rossendale

The Adventure Of Slimatron

Slimatron was walking on his sticky and stretchy feet. He was being chased by his enemies. They were after him. They were very fast but he was fast too. They were very hard to kill because they were invisible. They were called the dark ghosts.
There were seven hundred of them and just one of him. He kept shooting his laser eyes. Then he realised that he was in space. He looked around. 'This is not my home - Monster Mystery.' Then he got on his monster plane.
Two weeks later he got back to his home.

Harry Dolan (7)
Helmshore Primary School, Rossendale

The Queen Of Fear

The queen turned around, her red wings were glowing. She took her crown off to go to sleep. Just then she heard the gates open to her palace, she opened the curtains to her room. She looked out of her window. Her blue fur felt like there were caterpillars in her tummy. She stared out of her window. She had realised that her enemies had escaped. She ran out of her palace. She said, 'I will get you.' With her invisible powers she caught Clarea and she put her back in the cage and she never, ever got out again.

Poppy Di-Anne Mottershead (7)
Helmshore Primary School, Rossendale

The Earth Battle

A long, long time ago, deep under the Earth's surface, lived a creature called Zanton. He has legs like a gorilla, teeth like a vampire, cape like a magician and one large, bulging eye. Zantor has been planning his revenge for a long time on Spling and Splang. Splang and Spling travelled to Planet Earth and had a gigantic battle. Between them they both got really angry with each other. In the end Zantor won the battle and was really happy with himself. He won by lasering his animal, his animal ran away from him.

Joseph Ward (9)
Helmshore Primary School, Rossendale

Horses Save The Day

Wingy was a weird looking animal because she was part eagle, part horse and part chicken. One misty night Wingy went out for a walk to a Derby race. After the race was over she started walking home, but suddenly she took a wrong turn. She turned around. *This isn't my home because Planet Bong is a wonderful place.* Suddenly she saw another horse and she said, 'Do you know where planet Bong is?'
She said, 'Yes, take a left, then a right.' So Wingy did. She lived happily ever after.

Chloe Lomax (7)
Helmshore Primary School, Rossendale

The Day Peepo Shrunk

Peepo was walking around some snowy mountains. It was a sunny day and he was starving and trying to find his favourite food, enderpearls! Suddenly he spotted some but they were up on the mountain which was thirteen metres high and Peepo could only jump five metres. Peepo started to think, he thought he should just jump off the ledge he was on, so he did, but when he landed on the second platform the Water Demon jumped out of nowhere! Peepo was so scared he fell off the cliff! When he looked down, he had shrunk!

Aimee Haworth (8)
Helmshore Primary School, Rossendale

Max Saves The Day!

Once upon a time, there was a green alien called Max who had super strength powers. Max had five red eyes, ten wiggly arms, ten curly legs with white toes!

One day Max was busy saving people and then he saw an out of control car going really fast down the hill. The car had an evil engine and was going super fast and wouldn't stop! Max flew through the air and with his wiggly arms and curly legs he used his superpowers to stop the car. The people in the car said, 'You're my superhero, Max!'

Jack Bobby Ashworth (7)
Helmshore Primary School, Rossendale

The Battle Of The Kinderlumper And The Snake-Like Cyclops

One morning the Kinderlumper woke up on the streets. He must have failed his mission. That morning he went back to his base, a cave.

In the evening he heard a noise outside, he went to check. *Bam!* He got hit with a frying pan in the face. When he opened his eyes he used X-ray vision to see who it was. It was the snake-like cyclops! He fired lasers out his eyes but he reflected them back and killed him.

Watch out, he could be in your bag, he could be under you bed and gobble you whole.

Lewis Walters (10)
Helmshore Primary School, Rossendale

Dug The Vampire Slug

Dug the vampire slug slithered along with his blue skin, antennae and small fangs. Later, in the kitchen Dug heard something, but slithered over his book carelessly knocking over a few knives. When Dug slowly managed to get up he realised a knife had fallen on his arm and was lying lifelessly on the floor. Before he knew it, the lump got bigger and bigger and changed into an arm! *Wow,* thought Dug.

Later that day he decided to do more cooking but knocked off another knife. 'Oh!' said Dug.

Jake Hannay (9)
Helmshore Primary School, Rossendale

Big Mouth The Great!

One day Big Mouth was just eating his stationary things missing his mouth, even though he has 12 eyes and a huge tongue which he can play hockey with!

He was chilling and heard the biggest noise ever!

It was... Bon Bon trying to kill Big Mouth with his marshmallow goo. Big Mouth was so scared he screamed, 'Fire!' which he didn't even know he could do !

It scared Bon Bon away, so now when he fights him with marshmallow goo it frightens him. Bon Bon stopped coming and stayed in Bong!

Meisha Gamble (10)
Helmshore Primary School, Rossendale

Mindbobbling Mayhem

As the creature flew, he came to a stop at an enormous hill. The creature was beautiful and majestic. He flew so slowly as he was showing off his wonderful tricks to everyone in sight. He was fierce and never seemed to stop. As he lay on the hill, he suddenly fell down a hole into a dull cave full of lava.

That night he discovered he was immune to fire and could now shoot heat waves from his tail. Surprisingly, his name was Zelta and from then on he enjoyed his life as any other normal animal would do!

Daniel John Schofield (10)
Helmshore Primary School, Rossendale

Stomper And The Scary Kids

One sunny day Stomper stomped through the green grass park. It was a beautiful day and Stomper was very hungry. He was on the hunt for delicious food. Suddenly, a bunch of kids were chasing him. He did not know where to go, they were getting closer and closer. Stomper hid behind a tree. The kids ran past so he came out, but when he looked down, he had turned into a twig! He thought he was actually dreaming, so he hit himself on the head and then he knew he was not dreaming, but what should he do now...

Naomi Curness (8)
Helmshore Primary School, Rossendale

Dr Cockroach And The Fluff Adventure

Dr Cockroach was the happiest creature in the whole of the galaxies. He was more or less a cockroach size. He was in his flying saucer, then he heard a beeping sound. It was his engine, he had a little meteor jammed in his engine. He got out his blast phone. First he tried 999 and it came up with the galactic police. Then his feet dropped back with his long arms trying to grab the gears and again he got out his blast phone, then *ring, ring, ring*, it was the rescue ship and they took him back home.

Samuel Zangoura (7)

Helmshore Primary School, Rossendale

Need My Energy More Than My Love

Pretty Ping Pong Ding Dong (but they call her Pretty Pong) was fast, she was looking around like a hawk and trying to find somebody to prank. But then she had seen a man, not just any man, the man of her dreams. She was running to him and Pretty Pong fell over and split in half and her other side was standing in front of man of her dreams. Then they fell in love and lived together.

One day she gobbled him up and got more energy and she could run really fast. Pretty Pong said, 'I'm fast.'

Amy Jarvis (9)
Helmshore Primary School, Rossendale

Flapperman's Crazy Adventure

Flapperman rattled and jiggled all the popping candy off the ground which all the guards had dropped as they plodded through the prison. As the time ticked Flapperman escaped... She flung herself all the way over PC Head Quarters, Zoggerlog! Ever been here? Everybody at Slither Stop Jail decided to put on a search as they had no clue to where she was. She flopped herself into another universe. It became a popping sensation. Ever seen Popping News programme? Would you like to watch it... Ever heard of it?

Madelaine Beecham (10)

Helmshore Primary School, Rossendale

Discover About The Mean Green Blood Bottler

Green Hairy Blood Bottler Dragon was in her house and then she suddenly found a bug in her house so she tried to get it out, but she got so angry she had nothing to do except poison it. She had very bad trouble at doing it, but she managed. Blood Bottler, that's what everyone calls her for a nickname. She suddenly chased the bug and fell in quicksand and started screaming and all the neighbours ran to help Hairy Green Blood Bottler Dragon, they grabbed a rope to help pull her out and get her to air.

Grace Wilkinson (9)
Helmshore Primary School, Rossendale

Zych The Great

Zych was plodding up and down in a little primary school, looking for bogies to eat. Suddenly, he saw his worst enemy, Ming Mong Mel. She started to try and freeze Zych, but she kept missing. When Zych turned around, as he thought he saw a bogey, Ming Mong Mel froze Zych into frozen ice. Just then he remembered that he had laser beams so then he got out. After that, Zych and Ming Mong Mel had a huge fight and they both got hurt, a lot. As they were fighting, Zych shrunk down and then Mel got blown up!

Alannah Pollard (10)
Helmshore Primary School, Rossendale

Screemy's Unusual Day

Nine years into the future was a crazy creature called Screemy. He lived in a rabbit hutch, his body colour was multicoloured. Out of nowhere, his enemy came and pushed him over. Suddenly, once he was pushed to the ground, seven eyes had fallen out. He got up, wobbled and had to sit back on the ground. In pain, he heard a loud noise in the air. He knew it was a bird! A little mouse had found all his seven eyes; he tried to put them back in, but he couldn't. He decided to juggle, he loved doing it.

Molly Kelly (8)
Helmshore Primary School, Rossendale

Seek Snorter's Adventure

With his huge, circular head and tentacles like jellyfish, Bobler Seek Snorter trotted along the path on Planet Ekobot. Suddenly Seek Snorter tripped over because he wasn't looking. Bobler Seek Snorter noticed six eyes came out. An eye popped out of his arm, then another one, then another. One popped out of his leg. He found he could juggle his eyes and play basketball with them too. He found he was a shape-shifter because he turned into a ball. Then he turned into a tree with big, large berries.

Harry Kendall (9)
Helmshore Primary School, Rossendale

The Mystery Adventure

Dave is a little cute, green monster with only one eye and a furry thing on its head. His friend called Bob kept him safe and protected.

One day Bob was ill and Dave went for a walk. He was always happy on a walk but at that moment he was scared. Then he saw a sign and it said: 'Welcome To Wales' and he was far away from Pluto. Then everyone said, 'Who are you?' He thought, *I have my superpower machine to fly back home*. He was so happy to see his best friend called Bob.

Neve Grady (7)
Helmshore Primary School, Rossendale

Garfield And The Catwalkers

Garfield was walking along his icy and very cold planet. He was very happy on his home planet, but he was worried about his enemies, the Cat Walkers. Their leader was the king of all Cat Walkers. Garfield was really frightened, he didn't know what to do. He ran around and around in circles, then he ran into his enemies, the Cat Walkers. He was sure he didn't know what to do. He kept freaking out and going this way and that way then he said, 'I know.' He bought a giant man.

Maddison Bleakley (7)
Helmshore Primary School, Rossendale

Spots And Her Adventure

Spots walked along the place and all of her body felt funny. She looked around, she heard a strange noise and things were happening. What was happening? Was a predator coming? An elephant was coming. How could she get away? With a swish of her tail she got back to her land and she went in her house. Then she saw something weird and it was a lot of elephants taking over the land. The elephants were very mean and wouldn't tidy the mess they had made but she got them out to clean up and be nice.

Alicia Holt (7)

Helmshore Primary School, Rossendale

King McSpiky Beard's Adventure

King McSpiky Beard is a very spiky ball and whenever he gets angry all of his spikes fly off and shoot everything in his path! On a hot sunny day, McSpiky Beard went for a walk in a local park to go skate-boarding with his other king friends. Suddenly he saw his friends had no crowns on and said to them, 'Where on earth are your crowns?' His friends answered in a sad voice, 'Someone stole them from us!'

'Oh no, that's terrible, we have to do something now.'

Amelia Rose Watkins (9)

Helmshore Primary School, Rossendale

Bob At The Park

One-Eye Bob was lazy and he had one eye. He was covered in red and orange spots. He was very shy. He was at the park and suddenly he tripped over a log. He got up very quickly. His leg was hurting so much. A big lump appeared and he rubbed it but he was very dizzy. Every day it grew bigger and bigger.

One day he went to see the doctor. He gave him some cream but it just grew bigger. And suddenly one day something appeared, it was another leg, he thought, *This is from falling over!*

Phoebe Grace (8)

Helmshore Primary School, Rossendale

The Crazy Creature!

Once upon a time lived Steven Penn. He was huge, pink and fluffy, he had seven carrot noses and a hundred eyes!

One day he decided to go and see his friends on Planet Boggy Pencil, but his spaceship took him to Planet Ogg Bog, Planet Ogg Bog wasn't like Planet Boggy Pencil, it was rocky and absolutely freezing. Steven Penn's feet were very cold as it was very icy on the ground. But he made some new friends who gave him some socks made of slime, they kept his feet snuggly and warm.

Evie Robinson (8)

Helmshore Primary School, Rossendale

Bon Bon And The Marshmallow Thief!

Bon Bon was eating marshmallows when he suddenly needed a drink so he went to get a drink. When he came back there was only one marshmallow left! Bon Bon was very sad so he went to find out who took his marshmallow. Bon Bon had a brother called Ching and Bon Bon asked him if he had seen anyone with marshmallows. Ching had his mouth full so Bon Bon asked what was in Ching's mouth. When Ching opened his mouth marshmallow goo came out and Bon Bon realised it was Ching! Bon Bon was really sad.

Poppy Savage (9)

Helmshore Primary School, Rossendale

The Barcelona Dino

As Dino Fireball walked out on to the Nou Camp he was hoping for a win today. With 80,000 people watching, this would be his toughest match yet! Things weren't going to plan. At half-time they were losing 3-0! After a boring half-time, as they trudged back out onto the pitch, a transformation began to happen! Dino started to turn into a big, scaly dinosaur! Watching this, one of the players on the other team blasted a ball so hard it turned into a fireball and blew Dino up! Was he gone?

Harry Dean (9)

Helmshore Primary School, Rossendale

Blue Face Wins

Blue Face is blue, orange and green, he has teeth as sharp as a razor blade. However, there's a problem, he's lost in the ocean. Blue Face found a friend and asked him to lead him back to his house and they struggled to find his home, so both of them were lost. Then they saw a big thing coming towards them. It was a friend of theirs. So they all tried to get Blue Face home, but it still didn't work. They found another friend and then they all tried to find his home and they did.

Lewis Alderson (8)
Helmshore Primary School, Rossendale

Fluffy Face Adventure

Fluffy Face is a caring monster. She has black fangs, pink body of fur and purple hands with a black moustache and beard. She had landed in a crazy jungle. It was full of crazy animals. A cat came towards her. She screamed, 'Help! Help! I want to go home.'
Then a fairy came and said, 'Hold my hand.'
The fairy took Fluffy Face home and they both said, 'There's no place like home.'
'You can stay here if you want.'
'Yes please.'

Ellie Jefferson (8)
Helmshore Primary School, Rossendale

Super Story

Candy man went to sugary Candy Land and ate all the candy. One day he met his worst enemy, he was called the one and only Dr Crazypants. So Dr Crazypants said, 'How are you?' But Candy Man just walked off. That was when they were enemies...

Dr Crazypants went home and thought, *How do I teach him a lesson?* So the next day he offered him some sweets.

'This is how you share,' said Dr Crazypants. Candy man then said, 'I want to share!'

Joshua Bailey (8)
Helmshore Primary School, Rossendale

Sewage Squad

There was a clown called Juggles. He had a massive red spotty belly. He was on a mission called Sewage Squad, it was to save the world. He needed to find five crystals. It was a deadly mission. They all landed on Earth. They saw a pack of skeletons. They had a big fight, it took a day or two. It was a big adventure. It was a long day, they had no food, no water. Everybody was so hungry. Juggles found a haunted house with the five crystals. They ran out with the crystals and went to Pluto.

Alexandros Berbatiotis (8)
Helmshore Primary School, Rossendale

Squidy And The Hawk

Squidy landed on the ground on his three long legs and two blood-red wings. His black body shivered in the cold. He looked around, it was nothing like home. It didn't have a sandy surface and it wasn't hot, it was cold. Then he heard a noise, it sounded like an animal. Then in front of him was a gigantic brown bird. He used his two antennae to find out what kind of bird it was. He found out that it was a hawk. He shot his laser beam eyes at the hawk, then left and went back home.

Harry Clark (8)
Helmshore Primary School, Rossendale

Evil Potato Vs Ketchup

Evil Potato sneaked through the planet cheese restaurant. It was a beautiful day and he was trying to steal people's money. Suddenly he fell into some ketchup, his worst enemy! He tried to get out, but he kept slipping back in. Then he felt like he could get out! In a flash, he flew out of the ketchup. He had discovered that he could turn into Rainbow Potato! Now he was Rainbow Potato he could think of something and it came to life. He thought of brown sauce and it smothered ketchup.

Isabel Carter (9)
Helmshore Primary School, Rossendale

Blazeorangeworm Vs Dr Blazerlollyworm

Blazeorangeworm was fast asleep in a classroom. When he woke up he saw that his enemy, Dr Blazerlollyworm, was in the classroom trying to steal an orange. He wanted it because he was sick and tired of lollies, lollies and lollies. Also he wanted a change. If only he could get one because he never became friends with Blazeorangeworm. They never shared each other's property, often they challenged each other but they never got along. Now things are really bad. Now they are real enemies.

Natasha Greenwood (8)
Helmshore Primary School, Rossendale

The Four-Eyed Doomer's Adventure

Four-Eyed Doomer had four eyes, four legs, four arms and on the bottom of his four feet he had four springs. He walked for a bit and then suddenly he tripped over a road sign with a spring. A crowd of people came rushing towards him, picked the Four-Eyed Doomer up, then with a shock, they dropped him!

'His eyes have fallen out,' said one person. The Four-Eyed Doomer put his eyes back in his sockets apart from one. A person had pinched one eye so he hobbled into the horizon!

Tom Turner (8)
Helmshore Primary School, Rossendale

Evil Enormous Enemies!

The flying, spotty zorb's planet was wanting to bring back Santa. Sneaking to the end of the planet and consuming all of the energy he can. Off he went to Earth. Now he needs to make his enemies pay. He now wondered whether or not to go to their base, or wait. What do you think? He had to save Santa so he went for it and dropped a big bon bomb at their base. It surprised them but it did the job. The flying, spotty zorb got shot by deadly metallic acid. He was down but Santa escaped!

Carter Michael Travers (10)
Helmshore Primary School, Rossendale

The Story Of The Zingy Wingy Cyclops Fish

Once upon a time there was a Cyclops Fish who was swimming around in the invisible city where the fish from the city can only see it. He went out to the shops, he had run out of vegetables because he was a herbivore. But on the way he met Big Bad Barry, he punched Cyclops Fish in the face and knocked one of his eyes out. And then he found out he had x-ray vision but Bad Barry went to hide but Cyclops Fish found him and soared through the water to a rock and stung Big Bad Barry.

Henry Hughes (9)
Helmshore Primary School, Rossendale

Sludgy's Adventure

Sludgy was a big, beautiful monster with a shirt as pink as a worm. His hat was very colourful. Sludgy was not happy because his friends were on Doodooland Park and he wasn't. He did not know where he was. So he used his eleven super eyes to find out where he was. He found out where he was. He was in a jungle. Then he used his super high, extremely powerful jetpack to boost his way out of the jungle. Then he got out of the jungle and went back to his own really big family tree.

Daniel Cowley (8)
Helmshore Primary School, Rossendale

Ingoo's Job

Ingoo got out of bed making sure, with his four eyes and his gooey tentacles, he didn't have goo on his bed. While he was still yawning, he walked out of the door to the funfair. When Ingoo got to the funfair, Pongoo had taken over his job. He decided to dig a trap so he could trap Pongoo. Soon it was done, he squirted goo at Pongoo and he fell in the trap! Ingoo had a quick celebration and locked Pongoo up forever. When Pongoo didn't arrive at work Ingoo stepped in...

Henry McRorie (8)
Helmshore Primary School, Rossendale

Eyeball Cat

Eyeball Cat looks like he has bright green hair and lots of eyes, he also has a shirt and whiskers.
Out of nowhere he tripped over his foot while reading a book. Eyeball Cat found a lump. He was rubbing as hard as he could. Then out of nowhere another leg appeared. An evil man kidnapped him and took him to a jungle.
After a few hours he tiptoed away and while sneaking out his leg popped off. He ran out scared crossing his fingers, he hopped and got home safely.

Evie Harrison (8)
Helmshore Primary School, Rossendale

Capital Odonut's Adventure

Capital Odonut is a doughnut shaped crazy creature. He has six arms, a pair of feet and is pink and blue. He woke up, stood up and tripped over a stone. Somebody helped him up. He discovered that he had a lump on his head.

Then the next day there was another eye and that was where the lump had been. He realised that there were two eyes in the bush. So he went over and it was Icing. Icing had told Capital Odonut that he had a fake eye on. Was he telling the truth?

Jasey Hartree (9)
Helmshore Primary School, Rossendale

Zombie Bom

There was a very scary creature at Fire Land. He was called Zombie Bom. He lived in a cave close to the villages. He comes out at midday. He has green eyes, he likes to kill people, he has a bow and arrow and sword. He can fling his sword, also can not be killed. Zombie Bom can break their houses. Zombie Bom's house was made out of water in a cave, his favourite food is pork chops and vegetables and tomato. He has red hands, blue top and black, smelly feet.

Jake Bulpit (8)
Helmshore Primary School, Rossendale

Christmas

Once upon a time there was a boy who was a monster who lived in the North Pole. His name was Arthur. He had sticky hands and a long nose.
One day he sneaked out and went in the jungle. When he was trying to get a coconut he couldn't get one so his hand got stuck in the coconut tree. He could not unstick them but a man who could fly swooped down and tried to unstick him. He still couldn't unstick him. Then a strong girl swooped down and set him free.

Romilly Neve Doherty (7)
Helmshore Primary School, Rossendale

Greeny Gobby's Adventure

Greeny Gobby woke up and plonked along on his tinsy legs with his tubby belly, green skin and a massive smile. He woke up because he had a nightmare. Suddenly he realised he was in a different land, Turnip Tornado Land. Just then, he noticed the Red Rebel, he thought he was an enemy, the Red rebel scooped Greeny Gobby up and took him home. When they got to the Red Rebel's house Greeny Gobby found out that the Red Rebel was friendly and they lived together!

Isabella Dunn (8)
Helmshore Primary School, Rossendale

Mr Bong Fong

Mr Bong Fong is fat and hairy. He has a big tummy because he eats worms, fish, snails and slugs. He is extremely stinky. He plays games and scares people and fights other monsters. And he eats all of the animals and churches in Planet Bong and Planet Fong and Planet Pong. He drinks worm juice. He has dark blue eyes and a dark green nose and mouth. Mr Bong Fong has all different places to visit and Mr Bong Fong went to Planet Bong, Planet Fong and Planet Pong.

Archie Rowlands (7)
Helmshore Primary School, Rossendale

Big Bad Accident

Golden Slash opened two beady eyes that were rose red, his scales were yellow and orange with purple wings. He got up from bed and tripped downstairs. Suddenly he woke up again, he noticed he was in a shiny, dark place, his head and neck were hurting. A huge lump was on his head. He put some ice on it but it would not move. *I wonder why it would not come off*. Then he thought a new head might grow. He saw a new batch of marshmallows, they were yummy!

Mina Alice Boland (9)
Helmshore Primary School, Rossendale

This Is About My Crazy Creature Zombie

Zombie landed on Zombie Island, he hated zombies around him. He punched them but he got kicked and fell in a hole. It was filled with spiders and snakes and it was dark and scary. He was dead but he wasn't dead because he was a zombie so he flew back up to space and back on his island, back home. But there was a hole in his planet and he fell on a star, but it fell down and the zombie went up and fell down the hole and on the same star, but he fell down.

Reuben Howe (7)
Helmshore Primary School, Rossendale

Ball McBat And Ball Beetle

Ball McBat was a light green, crazy creature who loved to soar through the great, blue sky with his graceful wings.

One rainy night Ball McBat was hunting for a ball beetle because they died in the rain. Suddenly, he crashed into the deep blue ocean and he couldn't swim but the craziest thing happened to his feet, they felt like webbed feet, he clambered out of the ocean and looked down at the bottom half of his body, he had turned into a fish...

Evie Hargreaves (8)

Helmshore Primary School, Rossendale

Zizzle's Adventure

Zizzle had a super round body, and he is really orange. He has a huge eye. He woke up, went for a walk. He was looking at the blue sky when he tripped over a rock. Zizzle banged on a rock and got knocked out. He came to and he realised that an antennae grew out of his head. He didn't know what to do. Zizzle walked on. He heard and saw something special in the bushes. He saw gold! Zizzle grabbed it, ran back to his friends and shared it with them.

Joseph Claxton (9)
Helmshore Primary School, Rossendale

A Silly Dream

One time there was a crazy creature called Fluffy. She has big hands, big feet, eight mouths, seven eyes and her body is fluffy.

One day Fluffy was flying in her fluffycopter. She went home. She was very tired so she ate her tea and went to bed straight away. She had a silly dream that she ate all of the planet up. It was a very silly dream. She woke up wondering if she had a dream or not, she was being very silly because the whole planet was there!

Darcy Crook (7)
Helmshore Primary School, Rossendale

Mr Green Pants' Crazy Adventure

Mr Green Pants trudged along on his three robotic legs. He looked down at his emerald green body with his five eyes. A single eye bulged furiously. He had stepped through a door and ended up on Earth. He had been told what the bull's eye looked like and set off to seek his fortune.

A bit later he was thinking about the bull's eye when suddenly he had all the air sucked out of him. When he opened his eyes back he was at the bull's eye.

Alex Regan (8)

Helmshore Primary School, Rossendale

Crazy Cat Legs' Adventure

Crazy Cat Legs skipped into a classroom. It was a very dark night and Crazy Cat Legs was very tired. He wanted to go to sleep but then all of a sudden Crazy Cat Legs fell on the floor because he was lifting up some balls with his legs, then he woke up. He went outside. Something was following him. He bumped into a tree. Then tripped, then lost his balls, then all of a sudden Super Fox came. Then Crazy Cat Legs got tied up. He could not move at all.

Isobel Ball (8)
Helmshore Primary School, Rossendale

Moggle Wump And The Smell Trap

Moggle Wump slid across the stinky, smelly sewers on his jelly-like body. It was a gloomy night and Moggle Wump was hunting for food. Suddenly he fell into a trap... It wasn't a long drop but the trap was deadly. It was filling up with lovely smells. Unfortunately lovely smells poison Moggle Wump's brain. The smells were so lovely that Moggle Wump turned inside out for the rest of his life. But fortunately he managed to get out of the trap.

Fred Hardwick (8)
Helmshore Primary School, Rossendale

Bogy Brain's New Eye

Once there was a crazy creature called Bogy Brain.
He was half and half. One half is a clown, the other
is an alien.

One day Bogy Brain tripped up because there was
a ginormous log in the way. Then he quickly
hobbled up and noticed he had a little lump on his
head. It kept getting bigger and bigger. Until he
tripped over another log and the lump turned into
an eye. Then he discovered his new eye could pop
out. Also he could juggle with it.

Ocean Summer Flanagan (8)

Helmshore Primary School, Rossendale

Tom's Big Life

Skin as purple as a plum, and he's got too many eyes to count.
One day he went on holiday, and one of his eyes grew as bright as the sun. Then he blasted off to the sun, but the people that lived on the sun didn't like him so they tried to kill him. He made a new rocket, so he blasted off back to his beloved home, but what he didn't know was that his world was in danger. So it was up to him to save the world from danger.

Theo Francisco Madden (7)
Helmshore Primary School, Rossendale

Flump The Dump

One sunny day in Ice City when all the ice was starting to melt, one of the monsters had an idea to make a rocket to go to the moon. When there was a rocket, they set sail with big monsters. Then they all got in the rocket and back to the moon. They played games in the rocket and they had soon landed on the moon. They went to their house and they had tea and went to bed and had a good night's sleep.
Next morning they went out.

Mason Hitchen (7)
Helmshore Primary School, Rossendale

The Scary Fish Tank

Once there was a monster who had six rows of very sharp teeth and one sharp nose and he was called Blazer Robit.
One day when he woke up, he looked around. He had the biggest shock because he was in a fish tank. Then he looked annoyed and all of the fish were in one corner. Then Blazer Robit sucked onto the glass and it made a massive hole in the glass and all of the water washed him all the way to his home and he was happy again.

Aaron Kershaw (8)
Helmshore Primary School, Rossendale

The Return Of Sun Light

Sun Light was flying in his star ship. Sun Light has seven eyes, a star-shaped head, ski feet, fat sun belly, moon hands, one red eye. Sun Light lives on Pluto which is blue, icy and very cold. He was in the middle of nowhere and then his ship broke down. He went falling and falling and soon he was in someone's back garden. He saw a garage and it had a long piece of rope. So he got it and threw it at his planet, then climbed home.

Heather Scott-Bates (8)

Helmshore Primary School, Rossendale

The Burger Monster Is Lost!

Burger walked and walked then he came to a stop and he heard a sound. A roar. Then he heard, 'Uh oh, a lion!'
He ran and ran, then the lion was not there. Burger found out that this was not Food Land with his friends and food. He needed to hunt and kill for food. At last, he got some food; it was meat. He found some water and he had some of it. Then he went in a cafe and had some TNT. He made a rocket, then he went home.

William John Nutter (7)
Helmshore Primary School, Rossendale

Fire Burn's Adventure

Fire Burn plodded along a stony path, with stones breaking under his feet. He was scary, blue skin and had one eye, he was quite cold! Suddenly, he tripped over a twig. He rolled into a hole and didn't know where he was. Fire Burn was stuck! His tongue attached to a piece of grass.

'Uh oh,' he echoed! So he pulled and, phew, it came undone. *Whoosh, boom* and *bang!* He disappeared into the horizon!

Isobel Lorna Bond (8)

Helmshore Primary School, Rossendale

The Green Slopermon

Once upon a time there was a giant in his home and then something hit it, he ran outside and there was his enemy shooting fire so he shot all of his powers at him. The water hit him, but it was not any kind of water, it was melting water. It melted his little spaceship so he was never back again, but there was an army on the other planet, so he had them to kill now so he had to upgrade his powers to defeat that army.

Wil James Christian (9)
Helmshore Primary School, Rossendale

Sad Santa

Sad Santa dragged his small feet along with his Santa hat on, he had bright red skin and a huge head with a massive mouth. He woke up extremely sad because he was born sad. He decided that he had enough of being sad so he set off to eat Happy Santa. He used his special trick, shape-shifting. He turned into a table and ate Happy Santa in one mouthful. That was him gone forever, and Sad Santa turned into Happy Santa.

Jack Stubbs (9)
Helmshore Primary School, Rossendale

Crazy Creature Day

He likes to eat worms and snails, he likes to play football and basketball and swim. He drinks worm juice, he likes to play, he loves to make a bang but he wants a spaceship. He has a zombie ear but he likes ice cream. He likes ice lollies and chocolate. He loves his Xbox and his iPhone 7, but he just wants a spaceship. He even has an Iron Man and Dr Sparkle Man. But then his wish came true and he got a spaceship.

Owen Griffiths (7)
Helmshore Primary School, Rossendale

The Story Of Edie Aguer

Once upon a time there was a creature called Edie Aguer, he is half crocodile, half cheetah, he lived on Planet Fire, he was born on April 10th 1899.
One day he got caught by Dr Cheetah and nobody saw him again. One day he came back and then Dr Cheetah thought he should get him back. He spent days of planning, then it was finished, then one day Dr Cheetah came into the trap and they lived happily ever after.

Lewis Robinson (7)
Helmshore Primary School, Rossendale

Dr Spike's New Adventure

A long time ago in a galaxy far, far away, there lived Dr Spike. He was big and plump, a right jolly old elf. Anyway, he could do a lot of things. He could shoot lasers out of his eyes, he also had a fish and laser hand, on both hands.

Moving on to his adventure, he was just walking and then there was silence, not a creature was stirring, not even a mouse. Then he heard a big noise of a ship...

Joseph Simkin (8)
Helmshore Primary School, Rossendale

Duff Dun And His Amazing Adventure

Duff Dun slowly walked along with his tail swishing in the wind. His head was all over. He was now in the forest. Not looking, he tripped over his feet. He slowly got up and then he didn't feel right, his eye was in a different socket. What had happened? He moved his other eye into another socket. This is why Duff Dun always likes to make his eyes change sockets. Will he discover anymore tricks?

Daniel Clements (8)

Helmshore Primary School, Rossendale

The Spotty Clown

Jumping out of bed, Dino dragged himself onto his tiny feet. He had a chubby, triangle body with yellow skin. Suddenly he fell into the water because the crowd pushed him and because he was looking away. He realised that his spots had gone, someone picked him up. Dino didn't know what to do. He looked around and saw some clowns so he went to the circus with them. But was he a clown?

Lydia Jane Lord (8)
Helmshore Primary School, Rossendale

Wizzle's Adventure

Wizzle had a huge triangle face, three short arms and four stick-like legs. He was running along, looking at the trees, when suddenly he tripped over a crooked tree root. Wizzle bumped his head and was knocked out.

After a while, he came round and stood up. He wobbled, stepped forward and fell into a hole and scrambled out of the hole. *What should I do?* he thought.

Taylor Baker (8)
Helmshore Primary School, Rossendale

The Secret Monster

I woke up this morning and felt a bit queasy. When I went to my parents' room they weren't there. I decided to go back to bed, but when I turned round I saw my annoying brother. As soon as he saw me he screamed, 'Monster,' and sprinted downstairs. I thought it was one of his jokes. I did feel a bit odd though. When I turned around I saw a huge mirror with an absolutely horrible and grotesque monster on it. It was spotty with green fur and had wrinkles. Suddenly I realised that I was the monster. Nooo!

Vismaya Pillai (10)
Rossall School, Fleetwood

Zazzy Zanze Zooms In

Zazzy Zanze woke up with her antenna raised high, she could hear the sound of a fantastic music concert taking place. Feeling eager to find out more, Zanze jumped out of bed and stuffed her tubby red handbag with musical instruments; castanets, microphone. She shot off in her giant pink rocket. The flashing lights directed Zanze to the music concert at St Pius Hall. Zanze zoomed on the stage clicking the clappers of her castanets. Her dance moves amazed everybody. After Zanze finished her performance, she was back in a flash to her home, the musical part of planet Neptune.

Shreya Tol (10)
St Pius X Catholic Preparatory School, Preston

Zorgeret's Adventure

Whilst Zorgeret was flying in her spaceship she saw a new planet and flew to it. She saw the planet was deserted and decided to leave. When she got in her ship she couldn't see where to go so she took all the directions in space and eventually got home. Zorgeret was expecting a quiet evening but was instead greeted by her worst enemy. Doomster! Zorgeret cried, 'Leave evil villain or feel my wrath.'

'Never,' replied the Doomster and shot a balloon on Zorgeret. She got really angry now and shot gas on Doomster who was never seen ever again.

Maryam Bapu (9)

St Pius X Catholic Preparatory School, Preston

Curious Kiki

Kiki opened one of her three eyes and found out she was floating in the breeze. Suddenly, *bang!* She hit a clear window. Her purply-blue fur stretched on the glass.

'Um... can someone let me in?' her squeaky voice yelled. A rather tall creature opened the window. It was a human. Kiki crawled into the little room and saw more humans but they were much smaller. With an excited spirit, Kiki climbed on someone's desk and nibbled their worksheet. It was yummy. This was the perfect place for Kiki, there was nice food and no enemies from her old island.

Farwa Ali (10)
St Pius X Catholic Preparatory School, Preston

Bombshell And The Humans

Bombshell steadily walked down the road until he sensed humans. He ran as fast as he could but he wasn't looking where he was going and fell over badly. Bombshell had to dodge obstacles on his way back home to the sewers.

After a while the humans finally caught up with Bombshell and they grabbed him by the neck and strangled him, but Bombshell cleverly escaped and silently he found his way back home. After a while the humans found out that Bombshell was missing and they got really mad. Back in the sewers Bombshell was celebrating his big escape.

Edward Charles Greaves (9)

St Pius X Catholic Preparatory School, Preston

Bampop Gets Lost!

Bampop wheeled across the weird surface in search of his family. Then suddenly he heard a *bang!* What could it be? A purple figure jumped out of nowhere in front of Bampop. Before Bampop used his venom attack he went to get a closer look.

'Ahhh,' screamed Bampop, it was his worst enemy, Nitrag. Bampop spat out as much venom as he could, so much his mouth went dry. Nitrag squealed and squirmed as there was now a hole in his tummy. Unluckily Bampop was no match for Nitrag so Bampop ran and ran but Nitrag disintegrated him into dust.

Amirah Master (9)
St Pius X Catholic Preparatory School, Preston

The Long-Lost Creature

Torch trod along the long and narrow white road. His face was glistening with sweat and his legs were throbbing. Then he saw a colossal bucket. It was full of Torch's species. There were millions of little balls in the huge bucket. He started to climb, but he struggled to reach the top. He never gave up, he kept on trying and trying to reach the top. If Torch messed this up he would die. His hands at the top of the bucket, he finally climbed over. As Torch looked inside the bucket a strange shadow created darkness around him.

Rishan Ravishankar (9)

St Pius X Catholic Preparatory School, Preston

A Bad Day

Zid was plodding along on his two big, heavy feet. His soft, spongy body absorbed all the rain that was dripping down. He was tired and sad as he trudged through the crowded and busy streets of the planet, Earth. The atmosphere made him feel dull, as dull as a dying flower. Suddenly he saw Bully Bill! Zid's worst enemy. Zid ran as fast as he could to find somewhere to hide. When Bully Bill was gone Zid got out of his hiding place and walked onto the big, grassy football pitch. Then he looked up and saw a giant!

Aryan Patel (9)
St Pius X Catholic Preparatory School, Preston

The Dragons Next Door!

Beam Dragon was the most special dragon on Venus so all the dragons got jealous. Beam Dragon was flying one day and lots of dragons came to him and were saying mean words to him. After one day he flew into space and found a planet called Earth, it was the closest one to Venus. When he got there humans were trying to kill him! He said to them, 'I won't harm you but I will protect you.' After, all the dragons came to attack! All the humans made them leave! Then no dragon ever made fun of him again!

Hadi Bawa (10)
St Pius X Catholic Preparatory School, Preston

The Mystery Thing

Poggy went to open the curtains, when he found a massive thing in his garden. He thought it was a piece of junk that his garden eats but it was not. Poggy was too scared to go and see what it was so he called Plap. Plap said, 'Give me eighty cookies and I'll do it.' So Plap went and sat on the thing, he said, 'It is very comfy but I really don't know what it is.' So Poggy called the space junk exterminators but they didn't know what it was so Poggy told them to take it away...

Oliver Bamford (10)

St Pius X Catholic Preparatory School, Preston

Lulu And The Holiday

Once there was a shape-shifter called Lulu. She lived in Asda, but she wanted to go on holiday to Waterstones so one day she went to Waterstones. But something went wrong and she landed in Booths. Booths was like a hard rock but there were pools of water in places. Lulu walked for hours until she spotted another shape-shifter. She ran to him, but unfortunately it was a Minotaur. Lulu screamed and ran but the Minotaur was faster than her. He gobbled Lulu whole and that was the end of Lulu Smith.

Jonalisa Kubelabo (10)
St Pius X Catholic Preparatory School, Preston

Knot Again

A deafening silence engulfed the room. For them the party had just begun! Cautiously, yet excitedly, the tiny purple fellows heaved over to the top of Headmania. The Tangleteezers were here to get this party started.

'Ladies and gentlemen, please take your seats,' joyfully exclaimed one of the Tangleteezers, as a few were searching for hairs (with their long arms) to do skipping. 'You may start eating your yummy popcorn.'

Bits of crumbs scattered everywhere (dandruff). Served with Hyperpop (sugary blood). Suddenly Headmania erupted, everybody fell over and got tangled in the strands of hair. Unfortunately it was nearly dawn...

Aisha Patel (10)
St Stephen's CE Primary School, Blackburn

Alien War

Theop clutched his arm nemesis (Shoef) by the neck and banged him towards the ground. 'Surrender and you'll live to see tomorrow!' yelled Theop.

'Never,' screamed Shoef patting his back gently. Surprisingly something appeared. Armies of small, sparkling drones charged at Theop. Losing his grip, eight murky-red beams shot the army causing the drones to break down. Shivering with fear Shoef scratched his head frightened as to what was coming. Ferociously, Theop stabbed his arch-nemesis and brought him to his home world. Theop kept Shoef in a chest to remind him of how he had beaten his unbeatable enemy successfully.

Ahmad Phansa (10)

St Stephen's CE Primary School, Blackburn

The Monster Whose Name Changed To Captain Good Heart

One day, the fearsome notorious intergalactic villain, Captain Black Heart, wanted to start a laser war with neighbouring planets. His weapons were undefeatable.

The alarmed president of the solar system, President Unification, summoned his brave agent, Commander Hypnosis, to stop this threat. The Commander led a group of planetary agents with Supergirl and Spidergirl. They created a strong force field around Black Heart's weapons that stopped them working. Then Spidergirl trapped him in a wrapped web. He was then sent into a parallel universe where he lost his memory and became a kind man helping families with no delicious food.

Alisha Surve (8)
St Stephen's CE Primary School, Blackburn

The Adventure Of Shimmer Squeal

I live in Crystal Cove. It's quite peaceful here; except when my crazy brother Cailu comes running and screaming around. Mum and Dad have gone on holiday so it's just me and Cailu at home with Aunty Yazmin. 'Shimmer Squeal, come and have breakfast!' informed Aunty Yaz.
'OK, coming,' I said. I ate most of my porridge.
'Aunty Yaz, can I play outside?' I asked.
'OK, but be back before lunch,' replied Aunty. I went outside. Suddenly my shell-crown started shimmering; that only meant one thing. Time for adventure! A diamond castle appeared out of nowhere. It was amazing...

Hafiza Bhamji (10)
St Stephen's CE Primary School, Blackburn

Tease Me But You Will Regret It

'Ha, ha, ha!' they all sniggered and laughed at Betty.

'Be quiet!' screamed Betty. She repeated this several times and each time her mouth grew and grew. The giggling increased. Feeling depressed, she walked off. All of a sudden the poor creature had disappeared. She could feel mischief running up and down her spine, ready to flow free.

'Naughty Betty, here I come,' she whispered. Using her wings and invisibility she caused many catastrophes. Now she had became naughty and enjoyed every minute of it. No one teased her, however, she could not stop the mischief. She felt very undefeatable.

Aliyah Bangi (10)
St Stephen's CE Primary School, Blackburn

Gem Hunting!

One luminous morning a creature was spotted by Busterbumble Chops. 'Is it really the one and only, ultra rare Goldirox?' He got his net in action to capture the gem. 'I got you!' But he caught a cactus. 'Oh darn it,' he replied, repeating his actions.
Next he caught a moon orchid. Several fails later he decided to come back afterwards. He trotted to his tree dome. Did he really discover Goldirox? Whilst dragging himself through Crystal Cove he recognised a trail of pink sparkles, he carried on walking as if it was nothing! This time it definitely was Goldirox...

Aasiyah Patel (11)
St Stephen's CE Primary School, Blackburn

Griffin Shape-Shifter's Quest For Candy

Lurking through the shadows of Planet Invisible, Griffin Shape-shifter was desperately searching for candy. Eagerly searching, Griffin Shape-shifter lost hope. Suddenly he thought of a brilliant idea to fly to planet Earth to get his candy. Griffin Shape-shifter immediately hopped into his enormous rocket and blasted into Earth's atmosphere. As he entered Earth, he noticed that there was a party and the children had candy. The party is where Griffin Shape-shifter went. Sneakily, he shape-shifted into the cake then into the party hats. Quickly he stole all the candy and returned home to Planet Invisible.

Fatema Ibrahim Seedat (11)

St Stephen's CE Primary School, Blackburn

Titanath The Lord Bargainer

Like a chameleon, Titanath the warrior headed towards the Plutonian base.
'Flaming damns,' reported the blazing hero, 'It's barely 1°C here, I'm going to freeze!' He was ordered to take out the emperor of Pluto because he denied to worship and orbit the sun, Titanath's home. He headed towards the throne room and ten minutes later found himself chased! He had no choice but to burn them alive! He did that and was able to bargain. He found a lever which moved the planet and said, 'Worship us or else I'll melt your planet.' Their answer was ultra, super obvious!

Zain Ahmed (9)
St Stephen's CE Primary School, Blackburn

Ivory And The Wrong Turn!

Ivory stomped around with her two giant, blood-like feet. Short and fluffy with red skin, she was sweltering in the heat, as the sun shone on her. Ivory put her arms and legs inside her and thought deeply about how she'd got here. Suddenly she heard screams. It belonged to humans, hunting in the forest. They started looking at her and circling her. As she took her arms and legs out, she gave a ferocious roar and realised this was the wrong planet.

'Oh no,' yelled Ivory. 'It looks like I've read the map wrong, I'll never get home now.'

Rozmina Patel (10)
St Stephen's CE Primary School, Blackburn

Malt Teaser

'Ha, ha! You can't catch me!' Malt Teaser was on a roll. Six stolen, scrumptious chocolates in a row. Can you guess what they were called? Well if you guessed Malteser you are correct. Every six kids he stole the chocolate from were apoplectic whilst he was excellent.

As Malt Teaser trudged along on his melting feet, he heard some humans planning to catch him, so they could jubilantly enjoy their chocolate. Luckily, he had a plan to defeat them. Just when the humans were about to set the trap he arrived. Evil beat good as it did every day.

Fatima Ravat (9)
St Stephen's CE Primary School, Blackburn

Slither Speed Snake

In a land far away there lived a snake called Slither. He lived on Mars and had mighty powers which were speed flashes. He was of rainbow colours and very handsome.

One ordinary day he decided he would go on a journey which was to go and discover an animal that was unique like him and he could become friends. on his travels he met a strange creature called Hippogriff.

In one week they became the best of friends. Hippogriff was half-horse and half-eagle, what a fascinating creature! Eventually Slither had set off home and brought his best mate along.

Murtazah Shahzad (9)
St Stephen's CE Primary School, Blackburn

Competition For Enemies

One early summer's day, a monster called Furfang was up and ready to go to gymnastics practise. Furfang was half from Fur Land and half from Fang Land. She went inside her car and off she went. At practise she saw her two enemies, Cheerleading Woman and Karate Kid. She asked them to have a mini gymnastics competition and they agreed. After the competition they were so nervous to see who won. The judges decided who won and it was... drum roll please, it was neither of them. They were so disappointed. After that competition they all became very angry.

Aisha Usman (9)
St Stephen's CE Primary School, Blackburn

The Battle With Lugia

Groudon and Lugia hated each other. So they wanted a battle but the couldn't because if it's winter Groudon cannot go outside and in summer Lugia can't go outside so they decided, 'Let's do it in spring.'

Once is was spring they battled in the Colosseum, they did rock, paper, scissors. Groudon won so he used the move fire breath. It was a critical hit so Lugia had ten HP left. Lugia used shadow ball but it missed. Now Groudon had a chance to defeat Lugia. So he used dragon breath so he would not miss his slot. Groudon won.

Zaid Kara (9)
St Stephen's CE Primary School, Blackburn

The Story Behind Gas Head

Gas Head sneaked into his friend's birthday party remembering what his mother said. She told him not to enjoy himself too much or the same thing that happened to his grandfather will happen to him. His grandfather enjoyed himself too much and... she would never finish the story for some reason. His friend saw Gas Head sitting in a corner and offered him an eatable lotus flower, he ate the flower and couldn't remember a thing. Gas Head partied all night long and then Boom, there was a spark but no Gas Head. All that was left was a balloon.

Naailah Mubarakali (11)
St Stephen's CE Primary School, Blackburn

The Capture Of Zob

Talented Zob visited the planet Mars. She left Zobby to go and explore. Soon she discovered her enemy Crusher was also there. Crusher captured Zob and imprisoned her. Zob didn't worry, she could use her long tongue to signal to her friends and rescue her. Zob's friends looked at the sign and noticed that Zob needed help. They flew to her rescue and soon found her trapped. Zob asked them to grab her long tongue and pull her out. The friends were afraid of the suckers on her tongue. Instead Zob squeezed out of the rusty lock and escaped free!

Faiza Sheth (8)
St Stephen's CE Primary School, Blackburn

Mr Smellypoop's Journey Across The Classroom

In a galaxy far, far away there was a monster which was as tiny as a grain of sand. This little creature discovered an engine, somehow he took the engine all the way to Planet Earth. He could hit a toilet and kill an ant.

One dreadful day while the sun was shining high in the sky Mr Smellypoop decided to go on mission impossible. He ran across the classroom. He ran but children carelessly stepped on him. He'd suffered but made it. He got stepped on, played with and smashed on. This is the amazing Mr Smellypoop's fabulous story.

Safwaan Ravat (9)
St Stephen's CE Primary School, Blackburn

Frances And Krabby

One day at the royal palace two twins called Frances and Krabby were born. Their jealous uncle wanted to become king so he left the babies at the river bank, where a she-wolf found them.

Amazingly their uncle knew that they would come back to rule the country so he told the she-wolf to keep them there. For the rest of her life she cared about them, but Frances and Krabby ran off to a shepherd. As they grew older they found out that they were princes so they went happily, they won and ruled their country, Krance.

Zaynab Ravat (10)
St Stephen's CE Primary School, Blackburn

 Young**Writers**
Est.1991

YOUNG WRITERS INFORMATION

We hope you have enjoyed reading this book – and that you will continue to in the coming years.

If you're a young writer who enjoys reading and creative writing, or the parent of an enthusiastic poet or story writer, do visit our website **www.youngwriters.co.uk**. Here you will find free competitions, workshops and games, as well as recommended reads, a poetry glossary and our blog.

If you would like to order further copies of this book, or any of our other titles, then please give us a call or visit **www.youngwriters.co.uk**.

Young Writers
Remus House
Coltsfoot Drive
Peterborough
PE2 9BF
(01733) 890066
info@youngwriters.co.uk